Dear Parent:

Your child's love of reading starts here!

Every child learns to read in a different way and at his or her own speed. Some go back and forth between reading levels and read favorite books again and again. Others read through each level in order. You can help your young reader improve and become more confident by encouraging his or her own interests and abilities. From books your child reads with you to the first books he or she reads alone, there are I Can Read Books for every stage of reading:

SHARED READING
Basic language, word repetition, and whimsical illustrations, ideal for sharing with your emergent reader

BEGINNING READING
Short sentences, familiar words, and simple concepts for children eager to read on their own

READING WITH HELP
Engaging stories, longer sentences, and language play for developing readers

READING ALONE
Complex plots, challenging vocabulary, and high-interest topics for the independent reader

I Can Read Books have introduced children to the joy of reading since 1957. Featuring award-winning authors and illustrators and a fabulous cast of beloved characters, I Can Read Books set the standard for beginning readers.

A lifetime of discovery begins with the magical words **"I Can Read!"**

Visit www.icanread.com for information
on enriching your child's reading experience.

My First SHARED READING

I Can Read!

JUST MY
BEST FRIEND

BY MERCER MAYER

HARPER

An Imprint of HarperCollinsPublishers

To Gina—my true companion,
love of my life and best friend forever.

I Can Read® and I Can Read Book® are trademarks of HarperCollins Publishers.

Little Critter: Just My Best Friend
Copyright © 2019 by Mercer Mayer. All rights reserved. LITTLE CRITTER, MERCER MAYER'S LITTLE
CRITTER and MERCER MAYER'S LITTLE CRITTER and logo are registered trademarks of Orchard
House Licensing Company. All rights reserved. Manufactured in China. No part of this book may be used or
reproduced in any manner whatsoever without written permission except in the case of brief quotations
embodied in critical articles and reviews. For information address HarperCollins
Children's Books, a division of HarperCollins Publishers, 195 Broadway, New York, NY 10007.
www.icanread.com

Library of Congress Control Number: 2019932654
ISBN 978-0-06-243147-9 (trade bdg.)—ISBN 978-0-06-243146-2 (pbk.)

19 20 21 22 23 SCP 10 9 8 7 6 5 4 3 2 1 ❖ First Edition

A Big Tuna Trading Company, LLC/J. R. Sansevere Book
www.littlecritter.com

My best friend, Tiger,
is coming over
for a campout in my tree house.

I get everything just right.
Mom helps.

I am waiting.

It is getting late.

I am still waiting.

"Little Critter!" Mom calls.
"Tiger is sick
and can't come over tonight."

I am upset.

I am mad.

I climb out of the tree house.

I stomp across the yard.

I stomp through the house.

I go to my room.

I look at a comic book,
but I am too upset to read.

My little sister
wants to play cards.
I shut my door.

My little sister cries.

Mom scolds me.

I hug her and say, "I'm sorry."

I go outside.

I play with my toy figures,
but they are no fun.

Then I throw my ball,
but my aim is bad.
OOPS! I hit a window.

I ride my bike,
but there is nowhere to go.

I jump on the trampoline,
but trampolines are boring.

I want to walk my dog,
but he just wants to sleep.

Dad comes home.

He asks, "Want to play catch?"

"No," I say.

"Help me with the groceries,"
Dad says.
I help, but I drop the eggs.

"Dinner is ready," Mom calls.

But I don't want any dinner.

Mom says, "Sit down and eat.
You can't always do
what you plan."

I say, "That's not fair.

I'm staying in my tree house.

I don't need a best friend."

I play games by myself.

I eat tons of snakes and chips.

I drink all the juice by myself.

It is getting dark.

Oh no, I ate too much!

I am getting sick.
It is getting scary.

I go inside.

My tummy hurts.

I call, "Mom!"

Mom gives me
some yucky medicine
and puts me in bed.

The phone rings.

Tiger says, "I am sorry
you are sick."

I say, "I'm sorry
you are sick too.
You are still my best friend."